*The books in
the* Sparklers *series
are designed to give
pleasure to young readers
when, having achieved a high
level of confidence, they have an
unrelenting demand
for new and more challenging stories.*

Irmela Wendt

Baby Hedgehogs

Translated by
Kathleen Shaw
Illustrated by
Manfred Limmroth

Burke

First published in the English language 1984
© Burke Publishing Company Limited 1984
Translated and adapted from *Wo kleine Igel sind*
© 1981 by Arena-Verlag Georg Popp, Würzburg, Germany

CIP data
Wendt, Irmela
  Baby Hedgehogs.
  I. Title II. Wo kleine Igel sind. *English.*–(Sparklers)
  III. Series
  833'.914 [J] PZ7

  ISBN 0 222 01108 4 Hardbound
  ISBN 0 222 01067 3 Paperback

Burke Publishing Company Limited
Pegasus House, 116-120 Golden Lane, London EC1Y OTL, England.
Burke Publishing (Canada) Limited   *Registered Office:*
20 Queen Street West, Suite 3000, Box 30, Toronto, Canada M5H 1V5.
Burke Publishing Company Inc.   *Registered Office:*
333 State Street, PO Box 1740, Bridgeport, Connecticut 06601, U.S.A.
Filmset by Graphiti (Hull) Ltd., Hull, England.
Printed in Germany by Richterdruck, Würzburg.

Five baby hedgehogs
were fast asleep
underneath the roots of
the old dead tree
in the small garden.
There they were:
curled up in their little nest.

Jake came into the garden,
carrying his big saw
and his pickaxe.

He leant the saw against
the tree, which was so old
and dry that it had not a
single green leaf,
even in summer.

Jake swung his pickaxe
and made a big hole
in the ground.
He could see the roots
of the tree now.
Beneath them was the
little nest.
And five little hedgehogs,
all fast asleep.

"Gosh, you were lucky," said Jake.
"I nearly hit you with my pickaxe.
Never mind. Your nest is broken,
but you are all right.
Still, you can't stay here.
I must get on with my work.
I have some sawing and
some chopping to do."
He picked up the hedgehogs
very carefully and
carried them over to the
gooseberry bush, where the
grass was soft and green.

The grass was warm from the
sunshine and the hedgehogs
curled up once more and
went back to sleep.

12

Susy came home from school
and ran straight into the
garden to talk to Jake
He showed her the hedgehogs.
"Five baby hedgehogs
and no nest for them?
Whatever shall we do?"
cried Susy.
"Nothing," said Jake sternly.
"Where there are small hedgehogs
there will be big hedgehogs
to take care of them."

Susy went into the house.
Her mother had left a bowl
full of jelly and cream for her.
Susy put down her satchel
and started to eat.
"Those hedgehogs must be hungry,"
she thought to herself.
She poured some milk into a
big saucer and carried it into the garden.
She put it carefully
on the ground,
near the hedgehogs.

They were curled up close together
and looked just like
one big hedgehog.

They could not see the milk,
because they had hidden
their tiny eyes and pink noses
right underneath their spines.
The spines trembled slightly
and Susy thought that
the hedgehogs must be frightened.
"It's Jake's saw that frightens
them," she thought. "It makes
enough noise to frighten anybody."

When Susy's parents
came home
in the evening she
was dying to tell them
all about
the hedgehogs.
But her mother was
"rushed off her feet."
And when Mummy was like that,
Susy tried to keep
out of the way.
Mummy was talking to Daddy
and Susy heard her say,
"I just don't like leaving
the child on her own all week."

Daddy looked at Susy,
and Susy smiled.

Daddy said,
"But we are at home in
the mornings and the evenings,
and overnight."
"I know we are,"
said Mummy.
"But I hate to think
that she has the
latchkey on a chain
round her neck!"
"All right, dear," said Daddy,
"only one more day now.
After tomorrow you'll
be at home when she
comes home from school."

20

"I know," said Mummy,
"but a lot can happen
in one day."

"Oh yes, a lot can
happen in one day,"
said Susy to herself,
thinking of
the five baby hedgehogs.

"We could ask Clare
to come and look after
her," suggested
Susy's father.
"Ugh!" cried Susy,
"Aunt Clare always
goes through all my
things—she's *really* nosey!"

"John is coming to
see me tomorrow.
He's my best friend.
He'll come and stay
with me after school."

On the following day
Susy ran into the garden
as soon as she came home.
The saucer was still there,
but it was quite empty now.
The baby hedgehogs lay
beside the saucer, curled up
into a tight little ball.

"Have you drunk your milk, then?"
asked Susy. "You don't look
big enough to be able

22

to reach such a big saucer.
Perhaps next door's cat
has drunk the milk?
And where are your parents?
Why do they leave you here
all on your own?"
She ran into the house
and came back with the milk jug
so that she could refill
the saucer.

Susy could see
that the little hedgehogs
were breathing,
because the spines
on their backs
were rising and falling
very gently.

"Well, you certainly know
how to breathe properly,"
said Susy, who was
sometimes very wise.
She began to count the
hedgehogs:
"One,
two,
three,
four . . . . .
but yesterday there were five!"

24

The smallest one was
lying on its side.
Susy could see its tiny
face and one eye, which
was shut tight.
"He looks as if he's dead,
maybe he has
starved to death,"
thought Susy.
"Perhaps he has had
nothing to eat or drink
since yesterday . . . "

John arrived soon
afterwards and Susy showed
him the hedgehogs and
the milk saucer.
"Why aren't they drinking?"
asked John.
"Perhaps they are too small
to stand on their own."
suggested Susy.
"Let's lift them
onto the saucer then,"
said John.

"I shall have to be careful,"
thought Susy, "those spines
are very sharp."
She went into the house and
fetched two old rags,
one for herself and one for John.
Then she put one of the rags
gently over a baby hedgehog,
picked it up and lifted it
onto the rim of the saucer.
She dipped its tiny pink snout
right into the milk.
But the hedgehog only blew
a few bubbles without drinking.

28

John lifted the other hedgehogs
onto the saucer, one by one.
But they didn't drink either.
They slid from the rim
into the centre of the saucer
and just sat there, right
in the pool of milk.
Susy dipped her finger in
and realized that the milk
was very cold.
Perhaps little hedgehogs
liked their milk warm?

Susy went into the kitchen again
and warmed the milk in a saucepan.
Then she carried it into
the garden and poured the milk
into the saucer.
The milk was just slightly warm
and the hedgehogs seemed
to like it much better.
They paddled about in it and even
drank a tiny drop each.
And a second drop.....

But then they staggered out
of the saucer and crept back
into the soft grass
where they cuddled together
and lay close, like one
big curled-up hedgehog.

"Funny hedgehogs," said John.
"Other hedgehogs drink milk.
Why don't they?"
"Let's lift them
onto the saucer
one more time," said Susy,
"quickly, whilst the milk
is still warm."
They lifted the hedgehogs
onto the rim
of the saucer and they slid
straight down into the milk.
The smallest one
fell right over,
but none of them
drank anything.

Suddenly, the children heard
a deep, growly noise from
beneath the elderberry bush.
It sounded just like the rumbling
of an old drum.

"What is that?" asked John,
rather frightened.
"That's the big hedgehog!"
cried Susy. "Big hedgehogs
make a drumming noise when
they are cross. My mother
told me that!"

John asked,
"Why should the big hedgehog
be cross? Is it because
we have fed his children?
Perhaps baby hedgehogs
drink only hedgehog milk?"
"Gosh," said Susy, "if only
I knew why the big hedgehog
leaves his children all alone.
If only I knew . . ."

John lay down flat on
his stomach and looked under
the gooseberry bush
and then under
the elderberry bush.
It was quite dark under there.
He could see nothing,
except old leaves.
The drumming noise
became louder and even
more fierce.

Susy said,
"This hedgehog doesn't like
people who break up his nest.
And he doesn't like people
who lie on their stomachs and
spy on him . . ."

The children decided
to go back
into the house.
They had some cake and
some lemonade.
Then they played
table tennis.

Suddenly the telephone rang.

"Hello, darling, how are you?
Are you lonely?"

"No. I'm not lonely.
John is here."

"Oh I am glad.
I don't like it when you
are all alone.
Daddy and I will be coming
home a bit later tonight.
Will you be all right?
You must tell me if you
want us to come home now!"

"Yes, but . . ."

"From tomorrow onwards I shall
be home every day, but tonight
it may be eight o'clock before
we can get home.

Shall I ring
Aunt Clare and ask her to come
and stay with you when John
goes home?
Or when it gets dark . . .?"
"I'll switch on the lights
when it gets dark," said Susy.
"Are you sure
you'll be all right?"
"Of course, I will! 'Bye, Mummy!
Give my love to Daddy . . ."

"Let's play 'Mother and Father' now,"
said Susy.
"You can be Daddy and I will
be Mummy. I'll pretend to
be 'rushed off my feet'."
"And who plays the child?"
"Well, we'll pretend the child
is sitting in the armchair,
reading a book.
We can stand a book
on the armchair and
it will look just as if
a child is sitting there, reading.
Right, let's start!"
"Tell me dear,"
said the pretend father,
"why are you always in
such a rush?"

40

"You ask me *that?*
I'm always rushed off my feet
because I have to work twice
as hard as you and I always
worry when our little girl is
on her own. You just have
no feeling for children . . ."
"Of course I have a feeling
for children!
Our daughter is not alone:
John is with her and they
are playing together."

Susy said, "Come on,
let's put a book into
the other chair. Then
our boy can be reading as well.
They are reading about
large and small hedgehogs . . .
Wait a minute, John,
I'll fetch my own
wildlife book."
"All right," said John.
"We can read about hedgehogs."
It didn't take long for
Susy to find her book.
"Here you are, John.
There's a lot here
about hedgehogs."

"Gosh, what small print,"
said John.
"If I read anything at all
I shall only want to read
about two words, like those
here, underneath the picture:

'NOCTURNAL ANIMALS'
What are nocturnal animals?
Are they different from
other animals?"
"Well, we sleep at night,"
said Susy, "but nocturnal
animals don't. I know,
because my father told me!"
"Don't hedgehogs sleep at
night? You mean they sleep
all day long?"

"Nearly all day long . . ."
said Susy, and at that moment
the telephone rang again.
Susy lifted the receiver.
"Yes, this is Susy.
John is here . . .
Come on, John, your mother
wants to talk to you."
"Hello, Mum, yes . . . yes . . .
we are having a lovely time . . .
What did you say? Dad wants
to take me into town?
Yes! I'll come at once . . ."

John replaced the receiver and said,
"What a pity! I shall have to go home.
Will you be scared all on your own?"
Susy began to sing:
"I am scared!
You are scared!
Why on earth should
we be scared?"

Then she said
Ask me something else!"
And then,
"No, don't ask me another!
Go home to your mother!
I'll take a book off the shelf
and read to myself!"
John was a bit confused
as he went to the door.

"Bye-bye, John!
Hurry up, or your father
will come and fetch you!"
"Cheerio, Susy," said John.
At the gate he stopped.

46

He looked a bit thoughtful
and then he asked,
"May I use your telephone, please?"
"Of course you can!
Do you know the number you want?"
"Yes, I know the number.
John dialled the number.
"Hello, Mum! I forgot
something . . . I mean,
what I want to say is—
Susy is all alone here
and I shall have to stay
with her. What did you say?
Yeees, I'll ring you later.
'Bye for now . . .!"
"Come on, Susy, let's
go and visit those
nocturnal animals!"

It was not quite dark yet.
But it was no longer light, either.
Just in and between.
"I can hear birds singing,"
said John.
The children crept up to
the gooseberry bush.
The saucer was still there
and the milk glowed white.
No less than four
baby hedgehogs were
rushing about as if they
were running on wheels.
Susy whispered,
"There you are, they have
been asleep all day!"

"They must have been asleep
when we first saw them,
and we woke them.
Of course,
they couldn't drink whilst
they were asleep.
That's why they slid down
into the milk.
I don't think they even woke up.
But now they're awake,
like all nocturnal animals."

"I can hear birds singing,"
whispered John again.
"No, those aren't birds,"
said Susy.
"Birds sound different.
The baby hedgehogs are singing!"

Suddenly, there was a
rustling noise underneath
the elderberry bush.
Mother hedgehog came lumbering
along like a great big truck
on a highway.
She went straight to her babies.

Susy and John watched
very carefully.
"Look," whispered Susy,
"she's giving
each one of them
something to eat
out of her own mouth.
I wonder what it is?
Maybe she is giving them
some berries.."

The big hedgehog
went to the saucer
and began to drink.
All the little ones followed her.

A second hedgehog
came out from under
the elderberry bush.
This one was just as big,
but not quite as fat
as the mother hedgehog.
It was the father.
He ran straight towards
John and Susy.
He stopped
just in front of their feet
and the children
dared not move.

They stood stock still
and neither of them
spoke a word.

The mother hedgehog
finished drinking
and called her babies
away from the saucer.

She picked one of them up
in her mouth and carried it
to a dark corner
further down the garden,
where the children
could not see her.

The other hedgehog kept on
marching backwards and forwards
between the children
and the baby hedgehogs.
He was protecting his babies.
And the little ones sang and sang—
John and Susy kept as quiet as mice.
They just listened and watched.

It was getting darker and darker.
The children could only just
see the hedgehog
as she came out
from under the bushes,
picked up another one
of her young
and carried it away.

"A new nest!" cried Susy.
"She must have made
a new nest for them.
Now she is taking them there.
And just look at their father!
He is standing guard
in front of us
to make sure
we do them no harm."

"Come on John, let's go
into the house and leave
them in peace."

They went inside and stood
by the open window.
They could hear
the baby hedgehogs singing.

Susy said, "I think all five
are singing now.
Their mother must have carried
one away yesterday, but
we didn't know then about
the new nest."
John said, "We should have
followed the mother.
Then we would have seen the nest."
"Yes," replied Susy, "but I bet
they like it better when we
don't disturb them."
Then Susy's parents came home
and John's father fetched him in his
car.

The next afternoon
Susy's mother got out the big
wildlife book and read out
all about hedgehogs:

"The whole back of the hedgehog
is covered with spines.
Underneath the skin of the back
is a very strong muscle
which the hedgehog uses
to roll itself up
into a tight ball
whenever it is in danger.

The underpart
of its body
is covered with woolly hair.
Its young are born in
a nest lined with
soft materials.
Baby hedgehogs are white
and have no spines
when they are born.
There are usually
four to six babies
in a litter.
The female hedgehog
suckles her young
for about four weeks.
Then she feeds them
with plenty of fruit,
slugs and worms.

They leave their nest
for the first time
during a warm summer night
when their thin,
chirping voices
can be heard.
Hedgehogs are nocturnal animals.

They hunt for food
during the night.
When large hedgehogs are cross
they make a drumming noise,
almost as badgers do.
And, just like badgers,
they sleep all through the winter.
From November to March
they live off their own fat
in a hole under the ground.

Anyone who feeds
hedgehogs should remember that
some hedgehogs
love milk.
A few sips of milk
do not do any harm
but mature hedgehogs should not
drink too much milk.
All hedgehogs love fruit.
If you want to feed
small hedgehogs,
give them a thin soup made of
minced meat and tepid water.
Ordinary milk is
not really good
for baby hedgehogs."

"Gosh," said Susy, "we were lucky!

I am sure
our little hedgehogs
did not get tummy-ache
from the milk we gave them.
They fell asleep,
right there in the saucer
and in the evening
their mother came and looked
after them.
She came and called them
away from the milk.

The man
who wrote this book
seems to know quite a lot!
But he doesn't know that the
hedgehogs in our garden *SING*,
they don't chirp!"

"Perhaps he has different ears,"
said Susy's mother and laughed.
Susy said,
"No, he just heard
different hedgehogs.
Those in our garden were
happy hedgehogs!"

64